MOLLY TAKES FLIGHT

MOLLY · 1944

BY VALERIE TRIPP

ILLUSTRATIONS NICK BACKES

VIGNETTES SUSAN MCALILEY

THE AMERICAN GIRLS COLLECTION®

Published by Pleasant Company Publications
Previously published in *American Girl*® magazine
© Copyright 1999 by Pleasant Company
All rights reserved. No part of this book may be used or reproduced in
any manner whatsoever without written permission except in the case of
brief quotations embodied in critical articles and reviews.
For information, address: Book Editor, Pleasant Company Publications,
8400 Fairway Place, P.O. Box 620998, Middleton, WI 53562.

Printed in Singapore.
99 00 01 02 03 04 05 06 TWP 10 9 8 7 6 5 4 3 2 1

Edited by Nancy Holyoke and Michelle Jones
Art Directed by Kym Abrams and Laura Moberly
Designed by Laura Moberly

Library of Congress Cataloging-in-Publication Data

Tripp, Valerie, 1951-
Molly takes flight / by Valerie Tripp ;
illustrations, Nick Backes ; vignettes, Susan McAliley. — 1st ed.
p. cm. — (The American girls collection)
Summary: Molly feels that everything in her life has changed when her father
goes off to England to help wounded soldiers and her beloved aunt joins
the Women's Airforce Service Pilots. Includes a section on women pilots in the armed
services, and a project related to the story.

ISBN 1-56247-767-6
[1. World War, 1939-1945—United States—Fiction. 2. Aunts—Fiction.
3. Air pilots—Fiction.]
I. Backes, Nick, ill. II. Title. III. Series.
PZ7.T7363Mos 1999 [Fic]—dc21 98-34556 CIP AC

The
AMERICAN GIRLS
COLLECTION™

OTHER AMERICAN GIRLS
SHORT STORIES:

FELICITY'S NEW SISTER

A REWARD FOR JOSEFINA

KIRSTEN ON THE TRAIL

HIGH HOPES FOR ADDY

SAMANTHA'S WINTER PARTY

TABLE OF CONTENTS

MOLLY'S FAMILY

DAD
Molly's father, a doctor who is somewhere in England, taking care of wounded soldiers.

MOM
Molly's mother, who holds the family together while Dad is away.

MOLLY
A nine-year-old who is growing up on the home front in America during World War Two.

JILL
Molly's fourteen-year-old sister, who is always trying to act grown-up.

RICKY
Molly's twelve-year-old brother—a big pest.

BRAD
*Molly's five-year-old
brother—a little pest.*

GRANPA
*Molly's grandfather, who
doesn't like change.*

GRAMMY
*Molly's grandmother,
who always keeps the
cookie jar full.*

AUNT ELEANOR
*Molly's aunt, who
wants to do her part
to win the war.*

MOLLY TAKES FLIGHT

Here it is!" cried Molly McIntire. "Here's the farm!" Molly stuck her head out the truck window as Granpa turned in at the gate.

"Hold on!" Granpa shouted over the truck's noisy engine. "The ruts in this drive are worse than ever. Your grandmother's after me to smooth them. But I figure the ruts keep trouble out."

Molly smiled as the truck bounced along. Granpa said the same thing about

1

the ruts every summer.

It was August, and Molly had come to visit her grandparents and her Aunt Eleanor on their farm. Every summer before this, Molly's whole family had made the trip together. But this summer, Molly was by herself.

Coming to the farm alone was only

2

one of many changes in Molly's life since the war began. First, Dad joined the army and went to England to take care of wounded soldiers. Then Mom started to work for the Red Cross. Molly's sister Jill was a volunteer at the Veterans' Hospital this summer. Molly's older brother Ricky was never home because he had a job mowing lawns, and her younger brother Brad was going to day camp.

Molly felt as if change had whooshed through her life and set everything spinning. So she was reassured to see, as the truck rattled past the fields and the barn and the swimming hole, that here at the farm everything looked the same. Granpa didn't grow crops anymore, but he still had chickens, an old horse, a few cows, and a big vegetable garden. Molly loved the way the farm seemed to have fallen asleep long ago. It was peaceful and unchanging.

Granpa stopped the truck in front of the farmhouse. Molly jumped out and ran straight into the kitchen and straight into Grammy's arms for a hug. "Hello, Grammy!" she said.

"Hello, dear girl," said Grammy. "We're glad you're here."

Molly took a deep breath. Dad always said that you could blindfold him and fly him around the world, but he'd know the instant he was back in Grammy's kitchen because of the smell.

4

It was a delicious combination of strawberries, buttered toast, maple syrup, and scrubbing powder. Molly wished Dad were with her now in the familiar kitchen. The sun shone through the windows onto the white enamel table and made patterns of light on the shiny floor. When Molly was little, she thought Grammy's cookie jar was magic because it was never empty. It was comforting to see it sitting in its usual place on the shelf.

"Where's Aunt Eleanor?" Molly asked.

"Oh, Eleanor's off and away," said Grammy.

"As usual," muttered Granpa.

Grammy frowned and shook her head at him.

Molly was disappointed. What did Granpa mean? It was *not* usual for Aunt Eleanor to be gone. Every other year she had been there to welcome Molly to the farm.

Granpa pushed open the screen door and said, "Come on, Molly. Want to help me choose a melon for supper?"

"Yessir!" said Molly. She followed Granpa out into the warm summer evening.

★

By the time Molly and Granpa got back from the melon patch, Aunt

Eleanor was in the kitchen, setting the table for supper. Aunt Eleanor was Molly's mother's sister. She had short, curly hair and wasn't much taller than Molly. Aunt Eleanor moved in such a quick, light manner that she reminded Molly of a bird. Just now she swooped over, gave Molly a hug, and asked as she always did, "What's up, Doc?"

Molly replied as *she* always did, "Not much, Dutch!"

"Wash up, girls," said Grammy. "Supper's ready."

Molly was eating her second piece of melon when she said, "Aunt Eleanor, I bet I'll swing higher than you on the rope swing at the swimming hole tomorrow."

Aunt Eleanor cleared her throat. "I'm afraid I can't swim with you tomorrow, Molly," she said.

Molly was surprised. "But we always go swimming on the first day of my visit," she protested. "We do the same thing every year."

"Eleanor, are you going to tell Molly that this year isn't going to be the same as every other year?" said Granpa. He sounded as if he was cross with Aunt Eleanor.

"Now, Frank!" said Grammy quickly. She looked at Molly and Aunt Eleanor. "Why don't you girls go outside and count shooting stars? Your chart is in the barn."

"O.K.," said Molly. "Come on, Aunt Eleanor."

It was a tradition that Molly and Aunt Eleanor went outside to stargaze every night after supper and kept a count of all the shooting stars they spotted. Tonight they found the star chart and flopped down on a stack of hay. It was still warm from the sun, though the sky was dark now and crowded with stars.

Molly scanned the sky to be sure the North Star was just where it was supposed to be, at the end of a group of stars called the Little Dipper. She smiled when she saw it. The North Star had become very important to Molly. She turned to Aunt

Eleanor to tell her about it. "Before he left, Dad told me to look for the North Star every night," she said, "because—"

Aunt Eleanor interrupted. "You miss your dad a lot, don't you, Molly?" she asked. Her voice was very sad.

"I do," said Molly. "That's why—" But Aunt Eleanor sighed so deeply that

10

Molly stopped explaining to ask, "Aunt Eleanor, what's going on? Is Granpa mad at you?"

"Seems like it," said Aunt Eleanor.

"Why?" asked Molly.

"Well," said Aunt Eleanor, "I think because I've applied to join the WASPs—they're the Women's Airforce Service Pilots."

Molly sat up and looked at Aunt Eleanor. "You're going to be a pilot in the Air Force?" she exclaimed. "You're going to fly fighter planes and drop bombs and be in the war?"

"No," said Aunt Eleanor. "WASPs don't fly combat missions. They test planes, and train other pilots, and fly

11

planes from one airfield to another. They help the Air Force do its job."

"But will you have to go away?" Molly wanted to know.

"Yes," said Aunt Eleanor. "If I'm accepted, I'll have to leave immediately."

Molly felt as if the earth beneath her were falling away. *This dumb old war,* she thought. *It's changing everything. First Dad left, and now Aunt Eleanor.*

"What do Grammy and Granpa say?" Molly asked.

Aunt Eleanor shook her head. "Nothing," she said. "Your granpa hates changes. He says he doesn't fix the ruts because they keep trouble out. But what he really means is that the ruts keep *change* out. He likes being cut off from the world. He wants to pretend there is no war. That's why he won't talk to me about flying." She was quiet for a minute. Then she asked, "What do *you* think, Molly?"

"I don't know," said Molly quickly. But that wasn't true. She knew exactly what she thought. She hated the idea of Aunt Eleanor going away. She hated it so much it made her angry—angry at the war, angry at the world, and even a little bit angry at Aunt Eleanor.

Aunt Eleanor stood and dusted off her pants. "Come on," she said. "I guess all the stars are staying put tonight. Let's go in."

★

13

The next few days were long and hot and dull for Molly. Aunt Eleanor went off every morning before Molly was awake and didn't come home until supper time. Molly did all the things she usually loved doing on the farm. She collected eggs,

visited the cows, picked vegetables for Grammy, climbed up to the hayloft, waded in the brook, swung on the rope swing over the swimming hole, and one day even helped Granpa make ice cream. But nothing was as much fun without Jill and Ricky and Brad—and especially without Aunt Eleanor.

One night, Aunt Eleanor still had not come home even when Molly went to

14

bed. The night was so hot and sticky Molly couldn't get to sleep. She stared out the open window for a while, looking at the North Star, thinking about Dad and hoping for a breeze, but the air was heavy and still. Nothing came through the window but the raspy noise of the crickets.

Molly kicked off the sheets and brushed her sweaty bangs off her forehead. *This summer's visit to the farm is no good,* Molly thought, *and it's all Aunt Eleanor's fault.*

Just then, Aunt Eleanor tiptoed into Molly's room. "Are you awake?" she whispered.

"Sort of," said Molly. She rolled onto

her side and punched her pillow to make it fluff up. "Where have you been?"

"At the airfield," said Aunt Eleanor. "I want to practice flying as many hours as I can."

Molly flopped onto her back. "It seems like you've practiced about a million hours since I've been here," she said. "By the way, I saw two shooting stars tonight. You missed them."

Aunt Eleanor sat down on Molly's bed. "Molly," she said. "I'm sorry—"

"No you are not!" said Molly. "You don't care about Grammy or Granpa or me or the farm. All you care about is flying. You don't have to leave the farm and go away and be a WASP. You *want* to. You're going to leave just like Dad did, and I'll never see you, and I'll have to worry all the time that you're hurt or lost or—" Molly stopped.

Aunt Eleanor looked as if she might cry. She tried to hug Molly, but Molly jerked her shoulder away.

Aunt Eleanor didn't move. Then she whispered, "Good night, Molly," and left.

★

The next morning there were still a few stars shining when Aunt Eleanor shook Molly awake. "Get dressed," said Aunt Eleanor. "I have a surprise for you."

Molly dressed and stumbled down to the kitchen. Aunt Eleanor handed her a piece of toast and led her out the door to her car.

"Where are we going?" asked Molly.

"You'll see," said Aunt Eleanor.

Soon enough, Molly did see. They were going to the airfield. The big silver hangars looked eerie in the dim morning light, and the small planes parked in front of them looked as delicate as dragonflies.

Aunt Eleanor parked the car. Molly followed her across the pavement to one of the small planes. "This is the plane I fly," said Aunt Eleanor. "It's a PT-19." She patted the nose of the plane as if it were a horse she liked. Then she handed Molly a helmet. "Put it on," she said.

18

"We're going up."

"Me?" squeaked Molly.

Aunt Eleanor winked as she helped Molly climb into the plane. "Don't worry," she said. "You know I've practiced flying a lot. How much was it? I think you said about a million hours already."

Molly fastened her seat belt and

19

looked out the small windshield of the plane. The sky was brightening to blue now, and all the stars were gone. Aunt Eleanor spoke to a man over the radio. In a scratchy voice he gave her permission to take off.

The plane was noisier than Granpa's truck, and the runway seemed just as bumpy as the rutted drive into the farm. Molly gripped the edge of her seat as the little plane picked up speed. Faster, faster, faster it went until, smooth as a bird on a breeze, it lifted off the ground and climbed into the huge blue sky.

Molly smiled. She was flying! It was exhilarating—just like when she let go of the tire swing far out over the water, and for a moment or two she was not on land or on the tire or in the water but zooming through the air. She understood now why Aunt Eleanor loved flying.

As they flew along, Molly looked out the side window at the fields below. They looked green and tidy and well cared for. The blue river wound like a lazy snake past silver silos and red barns and farmhouses white as chalk.

"I never saw the world this way before," Molly shouted to Aunt Eleanor over the engine's roar. "I never realized how pretty it is."

Aunt Eleanor smiled. "Look at this," she said. She made the plane tilt to one

21

side and then swoop low. "Here's the place I love the best—our farm. It's the prettiest spot of all, isn't it?"

Molly looked down and saw Grammy and Granpa's house and barn, the vegetable garden and the melon patch, the swimming hole and the rutted drive. "Yup," she said, "it's the prettiest spot of all."

Aunt Eleanor steered the plane in a wide, slow curve and headed it back to the airfield. All too soon, the plane landed with a bump and then skidded to a stop in front of the hangar.

As Molly climbed out of the plane, Aunt Eleanor asked, "Did you like flying?"

22

"I *loved* it," said Molly.

"I knew you would," said Aunt Eleanor happily. "Come on. I'd better drive you home."

In the car Molly said, "Aunt Eleanor, I'm sorry I said all those things last night. I was angry. But I understand things better now. I can see why you love flying.

23

And I can see that you still love the farm."

"The farm is my home," said Aunt Eleanor. "It's the place I'll always come back to." She patted Molly's leg. "And you know, all those things you said last night helped me understand better how Grammy and Granpa must feel. I'm flying off, and they're left behind with nothing else at all to do but worry."

Just then they turned into the rutted drive and hit a hole so big Molly was nearly jounced off her seat. "Well," said Molly with a grin. "Not exactly nothing else at all to do."

★

Grammy and Granpa were on the

24

porch waiting for them. "Where on earth have you been?" Grammy asked.

"No place on earth," answered Molly. "We were flying! Aunt Eleanor took me up in her plane."

"Eleanor!" exclaimed Granpa. "What were you thinking of, taking the child up in that contraption?"

"Oh, it was wonderful, Granpa!" said Molly. "Aunt Eleanor flew us right over the farm. You should see it from up there. It looks so small and perfect. The farm is Aunt Eleanor's North Star."

"Her what?" asked Granpa, surprised. He and Grammy and Aunt Eleanor looked at Molly with interest.

"The farm is Aunt Eleanor's North

Star," Molly said eagerly. "You see, when Dad was about to leave for the war, I was really sad. One night we went outside, and Dad pointed out the North Star. He said in olden times sailors used the North Star to guide them because they could always find it. They could trust it to be shining brightly at the end of the Little Dipper."

"How's that like the farm?" asked Granpa.

Molly went on. "Dad said we all need a North Star, something we can find even when we're lost, something we can depend on to be the same no matter where we wander. He said that Mom and Jill and Ricky and Brad and I had to be

26

his North Star when he went off to the war. Even if he couldn't see us, he'd know we were in place. He'd picture us at home and know we were waiting for him, so he'd never feel lost."

Aunt Eleanor put her arm around Molly's shoulders and gave a little squeeze. "You're right, Molly," she said.

27

"That *is* how I feel about the farm." She looked at Grammy and Granpa and asked gently, "Will you be my North Star when I go away?"

Grammy's eyes were full of tears. Granpa's voice was sad when he said, "Your mother and I don't want you to go, Eleanor. But we can see you are bound and determined."

"Dad—" Aunt Eleanor began.

Granpa continued. "You do what you feel you have to do," he said. "Your mother and I will be proud to stay here and be your North Star if that will help you come back home to us safe and sound after the war."

Aunt Eleanor hugged him. "Thanks,

Dad," she said. She hugged Grammy, too. Then she turned to Molly and said, "I sure am glad you took that ride with me in the airplane today."

Granpa grinned. "Speaking of rides," he said, "I'm thinking maybe the time has come to smooth those ruts out of the driveway. I'm going to drive to town to get a load of gravel. Anybody want to go for one last bumpy ride with me?"

Molly, Aunt Eleanor, and Grammy laughed out loud. "I do, Granpa," Molly said. And they climbed into the noisy old truck together.

VALERIE TRIPP

At 9   Now

My father liked to sail. He taught me about the stars, just as Molly's dad taught her. He told me that sailors in the olden days used the North Star to guide them when they sailed at night. I was always glad we sailed in the daytime, though, so we could see where we were going!

Valerie Tripp has written twenty-one books in The American Girls Collection, including six about Molly.

LOOKING
BACK
1944

A Peek Into the Past

**FLYING
IN
1944**

World War Two was a time when

*An airforce pilot
in 1943*

most Americans shared a wish to help their country. Children like Molly held scrap drives and bought War Stamps. American men volunteered to fight. They became soldiers, pilots, and sailors. American women filled the office and factory jobs that the men left behind.

Some women, however, wanted to do more than work in an office or factory.

32

These women were teachers, secretaries, and mothers who shared a love of flying. So, like Molly's Aunt Eleanor, they joined the WASPs, the Women's Airforce Service Pilots.

The WASPs were the first group of women pilots to fly for the armed forces. They were organized in 1942, and Jacqueline Cochran was the director of the pilots.

Jacqueline Cochran was one of the most famous women flyers of her lifetime. She received the trophy for outstanding woman flier in the world

Jacqueline Cochran in her WASP uniform

Jacqueline Cochran in the cockpit of a World War Two fighter plane

three years in a row and set over 200 flying records. She had suggested the idea of an organization of women fliers to First Lady Eleanor Roosevelt in 1939. Together, with the chief of the Army Air Corps, they formed the WASPs three years later.

During World War Two, over 25,000 women applied to be WASPs. Almost 2,000 women were accepted and began training to become pilots.

When the women arrived at the

airfield they were issued flight gear and a uniform. Because there was not a uniform for women, they had to wear the same thing the men wore, a pair of coveralls.

The coveralls were issued in large men's sizes and were too big for the women pilots. The women nicknamed them "zoot suits." To make them fit, women had to roll up the sleeves and

WASP trainees in their "zoot suits"

pant legs and belt the suits at the waist. They were hard to wash, too. Women wore them in the shower, lathered them up with soap, and scrubbed them with a brush.

The suits had one good thing—a built-in notepad. There was a patch over the right knee that the women used to record their takeoff and landing times.

After seven months of training, more than a thousand of the women graduated and earned their wings. When they graduated, the WASP fliers wore "Fifinella" patches on their jackets. Walt Disney artists designed the fairy Fifinella. She was supposed

Fifinella was the WASPs' mascot and good-luck charm.

to protect the fliers from danger.

WASP pilots didn't fly in foreign countries and weren't allowed to fly in battle. Instead, they flew people and equipment to and from airfields across America.

The women did take risks, though. WASP fliers towed targets behind their planes to help male pilots practice their shooting. The men used

WASP pilots returning from a flying mission

real guns, and accidents did happen. Also, some planes the women pilots tested crashed. In all, 38 WASP fliers died while serving their country.

The women pilots also had a lot to prove. Many men did not believe that women could handle large military planes. One plane, called the P-39, gave the women a chance to show their abilities.

Many people called the P-39 a

The P-39 Airacobra

"flying coffin" because of its high accident rate. One general suspected there were accidents because the men who tested the planes weren't flying them according to directions. He decided to let women pilots test the P-39, because they paid more attention in class and always read the directions for any plane they flew.

When the women tested the plane they had no problems. The general wrote, "They had no trouble, none at all. And I had no more complaints from the men."

The women fliers had fun, too. They sunbathed on the airfields, played Ping-Pong, and organized plays and concerts.

Sunbathing on an airfield

They also sang new words to "Yankee Doodle":

> *We are Yankee Doodle Pilots,*
> *Yankee Doodle, do or die.*
> *Real live nieces of our Uncle Sam*
> *Born with a yearning to fly!*

The Air Force ended the WASP program in 1944, toward the end of the

40

war. For many years, these women pilots were forgotten. It wasn't until 1979 that the WASP fliers were given the same honors that male pilots had received.

Women today enjoy careers as pilots in the Air Force. Their jobs are the same as the men's because of a recent decision: women can now fly in combat.

An Air Force pilot of today

AN
AMERICAN
GIRLS
PASTIME

MAKE A STARGAZER
Let your stars shine bright—day or night!

When Aunt Eleanor left to fly for the WASPs, she asked Grammy and Granpa to be her North Star—something she could depend on to be the same no matter where she wandered. Molly always looked for the North Star at the end of the Little Dipper, too, because it reminded her of Dad. When Dad left for the war, he asked Molly and her family to be his North Star.

You can see the Little Dipper—or any other constellation you like—day or night with a stargazer.

You Will Need:

Round oatmeal container

Tracing paper

Pencil

Scissors

Map of the constellations (check the encyclopedia under "constellations")

Tape

Nail

Hammer

Black marker

Construction paper

Ribbon, rickrack, glow-in-the-dark stickers, or markers (optional)

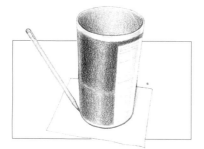

1. Remove the lid from the container. Place the end of the container on the tracing paper, and trace around the container with the pencil. Cut out the circle.

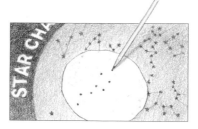

2. Choose a constellation. Put the paper circle over the map. Draw dots for the stars in the constellation.

3. Turn over the paper circle so you see the reverse of the constellation. Place the circle over the closed end of the container. Tape down the edges. Ask an adult to help you use the hammer and nail to punch holes through the stars.

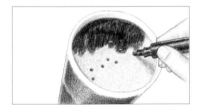

4. Remove the paper circle. Color the outside end of the container with the black marker.

5. Cover the outside of the container with construction paper, and decorate it with anything you wish.

6. To view your constellation, face a window or a light source, and hold the viewer up to your eye. You'll see stars!